BOTH
PUBLISHING

Published in 2021 by BOTH Publishing.

The author asserts their moral right to be identified as the author of their work, in accordance with the Copyright, Designs and Patents Act, 1988.

A CIP catalogue record of this book is available from the British Library.

ISBN - 978-1-913603-04-5
eBook available - ISBN - 978-1-913603-05-2

Printed by Ingram Spark.
Distributed by BOTH Publishing.

Cover design and typeset by Chrissey Harrison.

Part of the Dyslexic Friendly Quick Reads Series.

www.booksonthehill.co.uk

THE
HOUSE
ON THE
OLD
CLIFFS

Adrian Tchaikovsky

Other dyslexic friendly quick read titles from BOTH publishing

Blood Toll

Silver for Silence

Sharpe's Skirmish

Six Lights Off Green Scar

Ultrasound Shadow

The Clockwork Eyeball

Anchor Point

At Midnight I Will Steal Your Soul

The Breath

Sherlock Holmes and the
Four Kings of Sweden

The Man Who Would Be King

The House on the Old Cliffs

"Take the week off," Walther told me over the phone. "The whole week. No other commitments."

I told him I couldn't afford it, although the demand set the adrenaline going. Something was up.

"Oh you can," he said. "This time we've got a retainer," and he named a figure that was around ten times what I'd get for a week standing outside a club and knocking people over.

Everything about this case would be

different. To start with it was the first time that Walther had taken me along to meet a patron. Later on I worked out I was like a celebrity's entourage. Walther wanted to impress.

We went to a solicitor's office in Inner London: very impressive, brass fixings and oak doors and great stacks of file-boxes just round the corner wherever you went. The firm was Branmer and Stokes, but the lean old man we came to see was neither of them. The little thing on his door said "Alexander McLeir".

I had dressed up. Walther's reaction had been: "What do you call Michael in a suit? The Defendant." He was in his impeccable white, of course, an Englishman abroad in his own country.

When we went in, we weren't the first there.

There was a tough-looking woman with close-cropped peroxide hair sitting in one of the old-looking chairs, and a huge man standing behind her. His hair was shaved almost to the scalp and they both wore fatigues. At the door of any club I worked at, they would have been trouble, and they were probably still trouble here. The man was a whole size bigger than me, with a broken nose and what I reckoned was a bottle-scar down his face. The woman had her jacket slung across her chair back. Her bare arms were packed with muscle and she had an eagle tattoo on there that was a step off being Nazi.

In the chair to the other side of the

desk, which was as far as she could get from the two squaddies without actually sitting on McLeir's lap, was a grey-haired, neat-looking woman in a brown skirt-suit, clutching a handbag to her and looking nervous. Our arrival didn't help her.

"Mr Cohen," acknowledged grey, drawn Mr McLeir, indicating by not saying it that we were late.

Walther nodded and put his hat on the near edge of Mr McLeir's desk which again went pointedly unremarked. He took the middle of the three chairs, between the two women. I stood behind him, trying to look as tough as the big man.

"Introductions," said Mr McLeir briskly. "You're all in different lines of work. The

4

odds are you won't know each other, even by repute. You will have to take my word for it, therefore, that you all have a reputation of sorts. Ms Shaw," he said, indicating the woman with the tattoo, "and her colleague Mr Kelling are in the private security business, known as discrete and broad-minded."

They didn't look either, to me, but private security could mean anything from protection rackets to international mercenaries, and I guessed that discrete and broad-minded meant they didn't ask questions and didn't care who they worked for. I'm used to dangerous situations, but not so much dangerous people on their kind of level, and it was another sign that this case was shaping up to be different.

"Mr Cohen here is a professional paranormal investigator," Mr McLeir went on. I watched for the reaction in Shaw and Kelling and saw none. They just absorbed the information without a blink. That started to change the definition of "broad-minded" to mean people like us, who had dealt with odd stuff before.

"And finally, Doctor Furrisky is with the University of East Anglia's department of history, I believe, specialising in the late mediaeval."

Dr. Furrisky had been staring at all of us throughout. She was obviously not part of the same kind of world as Walther or the two security consultants. Mr McLeir obviously felt that some more explanation was needed because he added, "Doctor Furrisky has the advantage of knowing our subject by sight and correspondence."

"Do I?" she asked. "Mr McLeir, I do not yet know why I'm here with these..."

The solicitor gave her a thin smile. What he was plainly not saying was that she was here for the retainer, just like all of us. "I shall explain," he said. "Specifically, the man my clients are interested in is Doctor Liam Hendry."

Dr Furrisky snorted with sudden laughter and then covered her mouth.

"I assume the name means nothing to anyone else here?" Mr McLeir asked.

"Doctor Hendry the historian?" Walther asked smoothly. "Author of The Ancient Atlantis, Man Before Man and Where Angels Trod?"

"Very impressive, Mr Cohen." The solicitor tipped him the smallest nod of respect. "And of course, Doctor Furrisky is acquainted with him—"

"I know he's not a doctor, if that's what you mean," the academic said primly. "He's a very dangerous man, in my business. He writes rubbish and passes it off as absolute fact. I've had enough smart-alec students stand up and say: But how do you explain what Hendry says..." She stopped, looking shocked at her own vehemence.

"How do you explain it?" Walther asked softly.

"I don't need to," Dr. Furrisky said stiffly. "Because he has no evidence. He puts together flight-of-fancy conspiracies that would make Von Daniken blush and publishes them as if they were God's own revelations." She folded her arms. "So this is about Hendry, is it? Why should I even bother to stay?"

She stayed though, and I guessed that the life of an academic, especially one less published than Dr Hendry, was not a lucrative one.

Mr McLeir smiled thinly. "Even so, it is that Liam Hendry that we are speaking about. My clients have had considerable dealings with Mr Hendry," the concession to Dr Furrisky was duly noted, "And they find that he has not delivered on his contract. Not so very unusual, perhaps, but Mr Hendry has not communicated with our clients, or anyone of their acquaintance, in some time. Our clients are moved to believe that there may be... unusual factors relating to his apparent disappearance, and so they would like a discrete and expeditious investigation in order to determine what may have occurred. I should stress that it is entirely possible that Liam Hendry has simply fallen down the stairs or taken an extended holiday, but our clients are cautious."

And they have good reason to think otherwise was the obvious thought in every head in that room. There were such things as private investigators, tracing agents, professionals whose job was to find the missing. No one in that room was that sort. Something was up.

"You have each been informed of the terms of your employment. You have one week," Mr McLeir told us. "Please report to me all salient information that you find. If you find Mr Hendry in person, so much the better."

He looked from one of us to the next. Shaw and Kelling were without expression. It was a job and they were no more interested in it than that.

Walther would be smiling, and I could tell that he was intrigued, if nothing else.

Dr Furrisky was a woman very much out of her depth. She had been shifting in her seat ever since McLeir mentioned falling down stairs, it becoming obvious that the continued health of Dr Hendry was not of primary interest to the solicitor's clients.

None of us asked who the clients

were. We were after all, to one extent or another, professionals.

As it turned out, none of us was professional enough for this, but at the time none of us knew the gravity of what was going on. How could we have?

Mr, or Dr, Hendry lived inconveniently in Scotland. I will not name the barren stretch of coast his house was built on, save that the cliffs there were truly spectacular. Had it been less remote and windswept – even on the July day we went there – it would have been a tourist resort. As it was the, nearest little village, a haunt of sheep farmers and their support, was twelve miles away across pot-holed roads.

It took us the best part of a day to get there, which meant, in traditional style, our first investigation would be at dusk. Nobody wanted to be the one to suggest waiting until the morning, though.

We had driven up in an unmarked van provided by our security friends, with Kelling slouched sullenly at the wheel the whole way and music from the player that was so loud and featureless it was almost just static with a beat.

We had all got off to a bad start. Shaw had tried to provoke Walther first, telling him that he was a faggot and that she had shot men like him in Iraq for no other reason. Then she had started on me. I knew the drill from prison. Probably I would get into a fight with Kelling at some point, so he could prove he was tougher than me and, having seen him, such proof wouldn't be hard to find.

Through all this, Dr Furrisky watched us with a shaken horror. She must have needed the money really badly.

There were guns in the back of the van, badly hidden under blankets. I didn't want to think what would happen if the police stopped us, especially as Kelling drove over the limit all the way. I saw an open box with some pistols, and at least one thing that was a submachinegun or some sort of automatic weapon. Shaw and Kelling had parted company with the army on bad terms, and, apparently, with some of its kit.

Hendry's house was older than Hendry could have been. Walther guessed that some mad Victorian had come out here and had it built on the clifftop, for the view or the solitude. It was a two-storey business of dark brick, with a steep grey-slate roof and narrow windows. When we got out and cautiously approached it, with Kelling running ahead with a pistol in his belt in case of trouble, we saw that there was no more than six feet or so between the back wall and the cliff. There had been more, the dog-end of a garden could be seen, a suddenly broken fence. A fair chunk of Hendry's real estate had gone into the ocean a long while ago.

I went up towards the edge, but only very nervously. Heights are not my favourite thing. There was a mist on the sea. It would be grand to hint, here, that I saw something strange down there, but really I didn't, and I didn't look for long. I rejoined the others just in time to see Walther fall over on the house's big stone doorstep.

I ran in, thinking that Kelling or Shaw had hit him, but he was getting up almost immediately, clinging onto the doorframe and shaking his head.

"What?" I asked him, taking his arm. He looked at me a bit vaguely.

"The strangest feeling," he murmured. "Dizzy, very suddenly, as though there was a sudden change of pressure. My ears actually popped. Never had anything quite like it before."

The others were looking at him like he

was a fake, but I knew better.

The door was locked. Kelling wanted to break it down, but Shaw reckoned a quieter entrance was worth it, in case there was someone still inside. I should say that the curtains were all drawn: we couldn't see in. There was a window around the back with a broken catch, though, and I levered it open. Shaw had her pistol out now, and she slipped without a sound into the dark room. After a moment she flicked on the beam of a torch, and I saw brief ghosts of cupboards, surfaces, an antique-looking hob.

We entered Hendry's house by the kitchen then. By the time I got in, Shaw was already in the next room. There were no lights on in the place and when I tried a switch, nothing happened.

"I'm guessing this place isn't on the national grid," Walther confirmed. I had my own torch on now. Everything looked old-fashioned but functional. I turned a tap, and everyone jumped at the sound of running water.

I should say something about the shape of the house. From the front it looked as though there was a central big bit sticking out, and two wings to it. That makes it sound very grand although it wasn't any bigger than a pair of semis you might find on a decent estate anywhere.

From the back there wasn't the three-way split, instead the right-hand half, as you faced the back, stuck out a bit more than the left. It looked like it had been built by committee. There was some kind of stumpy little tower or something on the top at the back, but without decent light we couldn't see what.

I say this because, by this time, Shaw was back having gone over the whole place. "Nobody home," she said. "No power."

"Any sign of a break-in?" Walther asked.

She shrugged. "There's stuff all over."

We followed her into a narrow hall, and then into another room a little smaller than the kitchen. There were some cardboard boxes here. Two of them were empty, save for bits of packing foam; one was still sealed. Walther knelt by them. He had his white gloves on, I saw, to avoid leaving prints.

"The open ones posted five months ago," he said. "I can't read the mark on the other."

Kelling, with brutal economy, put a knife to the tape that held the box sealed, and revealed probably a dozen copies of a book called Where Angels Trod by Doctor Liam Hendry.

"Unless his publisher did him in for falling sales it doesn't help us," Walther snorted. "We need to get power back. Did you find a generator?"

"In the cellar," she said. "I don't want to warn people we're here by lighting the place up."

"Warn who?" Walther asked. "There's

nobody within ten miles outside, and you said yourself there was nobody in here with us."

In the moving light of the torches I couldn't be sure, but I thought she looked uncertain. I wonder now if she was as sure as she said, that we were alone there.

She led us to the next room, which was cluttered with cabinets, and Doctor Furrisky suddenly gave out a little cry of alarm. Instantly I heard safety-catches come off two guns, and I thought that someone was going to get shot out of sheer enthusiasm. The doctor was in the doorway still, her torch directed upwards, where it had caught a particularly unpleasant face.

It was a skull, and not a human skull, but after the initial surprise it was just odd, not scary. Hendry, for reasons of his own, had a wired-together fish skeleton hanging from his ceiling. It was a big one, certainly, a good six feet long, but it was still a fish for all that. I took the chance to flash my torch around, and found that the cabinets here had glass fronts, and that there were other things on shelves or hanging on the wall. It looked like a little museum.

"Lights first, look later," Walther said, and Shaw led us into the next room, which I reckoned must be the front left one, looking from where we'd driven up.

It had been done up as a library,

although a lot of the books were packed in on their sides or on top of other books, and I reckoned Dr Hendry had been needing a bigger room for a while. Shaw had gone to a hatch in the floor and now she paused. I had her pegged as a methodical person. As I saw her hesitate, I could read her mind from her body language. You didn't have to be someone clever like Walther to see her think, I didn't leave that open, did I... well I must have done.

We went down. It was a big old petrol generator, but at least it was newer than the house. There were spare cans by one on the cellar walls. It was the work of ten minutes to get it going, and it made a hell of a racket. If there was anyone else in the neighbourhood then they most certainly knew we were there.

The lights were on upstairs when we got there, showing us the whole overstuffed state of the library. Walther and Dr Furrisky gave the shelves a once-over.

"Quite a broad range of reading habits our man has," Walther announced. "There's reference here for about five thousand years of history, a stack of sciences, and every conspiracy about aliens and lost civilisations you can name."

"Hardly surprising," Dr Furrisky remarked. "I imagine he just took it in and spat it right back out." The trip had not warmed her to Dr Hendry.

The two security types had gone to

check the house over in the light. The rest of us went back into the museum, and stopped in the doorway, staring.

It was quite the collection that Dr Hendry had put together here. The cabinets had a whole jumble of things in them: from odd bits of metal like buckles and badges to bits of paper and whole costume-drama-style sets of clothing. There were some swords and old-fashioned guns and a helmet in one case. There were trays of shells, and two more fish skeletons, in cases and smaller than the big one above us. On the walls were maps and charts, framed and behind glass. It must, in my opinion right then, have been worth a fortune.

Dr Furrisky went over to one of the

cases, looking down at some kind of brass instrument. She was frowning. When Walther and I went out she stayed behind.

Most of the sticking-out bit of the front of the house was a hallway, and the exhibits started there, really. There were two suits of armour flanking the door into the museum, stood on stands as if the place was a castle in a horror film. One looked like the Roman soldiers at the start of Gladiator and Walther said the other, with its crested, plumed helmet, looked like Spanish conquistador. Dr Hendry was a man who liked to live amongst history, whatever Dr Furrisky thought of him.

From the hall we found the stairs. Kelling met us at the top, stared at us for a moment, and then went on about his work. Walther and I passed on into a big, untidy room dominated by a long table. There was a lot of clutter here, and some more exhibits that looked as though they were being prepared. There was a skeleton of something else, not a fish, but some kind of crocodile, that was halfway through being wired up, and a cardboard box of what I thought at first glance were washers, and another of shells and stuff waiting to be sorted.

"Look here," Walther said. He had found a case that had the front smashed out of it. It had a layer of stones in the bottom but for a moment I couldn't work out what it was. Then he showed me the staining on the carpet where the broken glass was, and I clicked that it had been an aquarium.

"I don't see any dead fish," I said helpfully. Walther touched the carpet, confirming that the spillage was not even damp.

"Strange," he said, and at my look he added, "Have you seen any other damage? The generator must have run down, but there's no sign of Hendry going anywhere, or of anyone breaking in. And yet."

"Maybe he broke it himself, cleared up the fish, never got round to fixing it," I said.

"Maybe," Walther allowed. He was not convinced.

I should say now that not all of these mysteries were ever answered. For some of them I only have guesswork, and some of that I will not speak of. But I'm going too far too fast.

I put my head into the next room to find it was the bedroom. There were no signs of any intruder going over the things, but something on the bedside table caught my eye and I took it. When I rejoined Walther in the workshop I was leafing through its contents: Dr Hendry's wallet.

"There's thirty quid in cash here," I said. "And cards, right out in plain sight. No burglar then."

Walther was grinning at me broadly, and I knew he had trumped me. "What is it?"

He pushed the box of washers at

me and I looked inside. They weren't washers. They were coins. They were all different sorts, but they were all unfamiliar, with foreign writing and people in costume.

"They feel right, for silver," Walther said lightly. "I reckon there's a couple of hundred in the box there.

"Is this... what is it? Treasure trove?" I asked thoughtfully.

"There are Roman in there, and others with the head of Charles the Second, and a lot in between," said Walther. His grin was still there, wider if anything. It was not the money, this little fortune left lying on Hendry's worktable: it was the discovery.

"What's going on?"

"We'll find out," Walther assured me. "It looks as though our Dr Hendry was a very, very lucky archaeologist, or something else…" He frowned at the coins. "Put them in your bag, will you?"

"Really?"

"I want Furrisky to look at them…" He didn't have to say that he didn't trust Shaw and Kelling with a fortune in antique silver.

"There are some stairs in the bedroom, by the way." I showed him the little spiral of stone steps built into one corner. There was a trapdoor in the ceiling that must lead to the stubby tower, and I unlatched it and pushed it open. Rather than revealing any magical little room full of curiosities, it opened straight onto the roof, a little railed-off square platform that overlooked the cliff. It was dark enough now that the sea was nothing but the sound of waves, and I was glad for that. The railing reached to about mid-thigh.

"This could be what happened to Dr Hendry," I said.

"Not unless he had a magical way to latch the trapdoor after him," Walther pointed out. "Besides, our man was a climber, in his spare time."

I goggled at him, and he grinned again, this time just at how clever he was. "The open boxes. They had receipts. Climbing gear, spikes, a rope ladder, a couple of long-life camping lamps, some of those chemical glowsticks. Suggest anything?"

"Caving?"

The pause meant he hadn't thought of that. "Well I was thinking of the cliff, but yes, sea caves... and easy enough to get stuck in one. You brought your laptop?"

"Sure."

"Check it out for me. Pop on the woo-wa. Speilunkers will have their websites. And find out about this house, if you can – who had it built and that. There's a story there."

It was late, and nobody wanted to sleep in the van. Shaw and Kelling commandeered the bedroom, and Walther and I took some sheets and put up on the sofa of the living room we found beyond the kitchen. When we bedded down Dr Furrisky was still going over the museum.

Try as I might, crawling over the strangled, patchy bandwidth my mobile could eke out here, I could find no mention of any sea-caves anywhere near where we were.

I was up with the dawn because Walther was an early riser and I couldn't sleep with him prowling about the place poking around. I used the time to make good my research: it took me a long time to find any mention of the house. In the end, an hour of image searching found me a grainy black-and-white photo of what was recognisably the house we were in, together with rather more garden than it currently sported.

The site was dedicated to Victorian eccentrics and said that the house had been commissioned by the gentleman scholar Sir Edward Fairleigh, who was involved, from the look of it, in any number of daft schemes, including financing an expedition to the hollow centre of the earth in 1898. He died in penury in 1909, according to my site, and there was no mention of who got the house.

We met up in the kitchen, making free with Hendry's toaster and hob. Dr Furrisky was there first, making tea, and she waited for us all to assemble before making her announcement.

"This is much bigger than any of you realise," she told us. When nobody gasped or asked her why, she continued. "I always knew Hendry was a fraud, but I'd never guessed he was a huge crook as well. This is enormous. We have to call the police."

Walther and I didn't have many things in common with Shaw and Kelling, but not wanting to call the police was one. "Why don't you tell us what you mean?" Walther invited her.

"Everything in that museum is a fake," Dr Furrisky said, qualifying it with, "Well, everything I'm qualified to give an opinion on. The shells and the fish and so on could be real for all I know, but I wouldn't count on it."

Everyone looked at her fairly blankly except Walther, who nodded for her to continue. She led us out, mugs in hand, to look at the two suits of armour. "Look," she said. "A Roman legionary?"

"What's wrong with it?" Kelling said stubbornly. "Looks all right to me. Looks like out of that film."

"That's the point," she said patiently. "Rome fell over a thousand years ago. Don't you think the preservation is a bit good? This is newly made. Everything in the museum is newly made. It very good. It's all made from the right stuff, but it's not been finished. Or maybe it's the stuff that Hendry kept back for himself.

Everything else would have been aged."

Still only Walther understood what she meant, so she forged on.

"There is a worldwide industry in forging antiquities," she explained. "It's worth millions. Fake mummies, fake treasures, fake dinosaur bones. Collectors and museums are hoodwinked into paying thousands, tens of thousands. It's become an art form. On a finished piece only a real expert can tell you it's fake. I think our Liam Hendry has been making his real fortune forging antiques. You've all seen the workshop upstairs. He would have made his pieces, and then aged them to make them seem just like the real thing, and made a fortune. Perhaps the people who are paying us so much are his clients. And perhaps being mixed up in this is why he's been made to disappear!"

The revelation would have been more shocking to the sort of people that she was used to dealing with. We just nodded thoughtfully. It was obviously a good racket if you had the skills.

"No police," Shaw said flatly. "We tell our employers only. Don't forget why we're here."

Dr. Furrisky looked upset at that, but Shaw obviously frightened her.

"Have you found anything else, Doctor?" Walther asked mildly.

"I… think I found his accounts," she said, looking sulky. "I don't know. They're in code or something."

"You look at them," Shaw told Walther. "Now it's daylight we'll give the place another going over. After that maybe we'll try the nearest village."

Hendry's 'accounts' were in a big old book which was about three-quarters written in. I mentioned that I thought he'd have done things on computer, and Walther agreed.

"But we've not seen one, have we?" he pointed out. "I'd guess that he doesn't even write his books here. You can't get away with a typewriter in today's market. So why are these..." He looked down the open pages, seeing rows of anonymous figures: six digits and then four. "You know this doesn't look like accounts to me..."

"Well what do you think it is?" Dr Furrisky asked, nettled.

"Tide tables," Walther said, flicking back a few pages. "These are dates and times. High tides and low tides...?"

His finger passed down the columns. "Too irregular, though. It skips days, or has three or four tides a day... Very peculiar." He flicked back and back, and made an interested noise. "And here the handwriting changes, and it looks like... nineteen seventy-eight was when Doctor Hendry started his calculations. Picking up from his predecessor after a... thirty-year gap. But what was he calculating? Michael, any chance you could take a bunch of these dates and times and see if the old woo-wa will recognise them?"

I tried it, at length and with as much poking and prying as I could work into the search engine, but there was absolutely nothing. Walther spent the time turning pages in the incomprehensible old ledger, and the doctor kicked about the fake museum making notes.

"There's nothing," Shaw and Kelling announced. "More of your fakes in the study upstairs, but no sign of the man. Clothes still there, shoes, suitcases. Plus the wallet."

"He didn't leave, or at least not intending to be gone for long," Walther agreed.

"Well then," Shaw told him. "You're supposed to be the psychic. You tell us something we don't know."

"I would rather take these matters at my own pace, thank you, Ms. Shaw," Walther said, not looking up from the book. A moment later she had dragged him up by his jacket and backed him against a wall. I moved in, but Kelling stood in my way like the side of a barn.

"Listen you," Shaw told Walther. "We're getting paid flat rate here. That means I'd rather be done in three days than a week. I have other commitments. Now do your bloody job."

"Well then." Walther, held up on tiptoes against the wall, managed a tight smile. "I assume you found the secret door?"

There was a silence that spoke volumes, and then Shaw let him down.

He made a great show of brushing off his lapels, like a cat that had been given a shock grooming itself for comfort.

"Show us," Shaw said. Walther smiled again and led us all into the living room where he and I had spent the night.

"What do you notice?" he asked. Shaw and Kelling stared at him, not playing the game. He sighed.

"The sofa is at a bit of an odd angle, no? It should be against that wall. Why isn't it? Because there is something there that someone needed to get to."

Shaw approached the suspect wall cautiously, running her hands along it. She grunted. "All right, there's a break. Get a crowbar."

This last was to Kelling and Walther

said, hurriedly, "No need. I think it will open, given the correct application."

She stepped back from it. "When were you going to mention this?"

"When I was ready. I prefer to be methodical when I can be."

"Open it then."

Walther approached the supposed secret door. From where I stood it was invisible. Closer, I saw a hair-thin line that interrupted the wallpaper and the plaster, but it was very well done. I thought about the way the house was arranged and whispered to Walther, "Isn't this just going to be the cupboard under the stairs?"

"Yes, possibly," he murmured back. "Let's hope there's something interesting he keeps there."

There was one of those raised plaster dado rails at about waist height, with different wallpaper above and below. Walther found a part of it that seemed loose, and he jiggled and fiddled with it until there was a click, and a section of wall became a door that slowly swung outwards. Walther stepped back quickly, and I smelt an odd smell, slightly fishy, slightly rotten, coming in on a gust of cool air.

"It's not just a cupboard," Walther said. Everyone was crowding to have a look. I peered over Walther's shoulder and saw – stairs.

Stairs going down. Stone steps descending into the rock of the cliff. Ten feet down and the darkness was pitch.

Walther's expression led the rest to be believe he had been expecting it. It may have been true.

To do Shaw credit she did not simply charge down into the black. Instead she and Kelling headed off for the van to get more kit. Walther examined the secret door, showing me that it was made to open, far more obviously, from the other side. Dr. Hendry had not wanted to get locked out, obviously, while doing whatever he did down there.

"Any ideas?" I asked him, looking at the steps. I had flashed my torch down the shaft, but the steps continued further than the light could reach. The angle of descent was very steep, and the steps were slightly hollowed and rounded, in use long before Hendry had found them. The walls of the stair-shaft were smooth stone, not the natural rock but solid slabs that someone had manhandled there to line it. It all looked very old. Dr Furrisky, who was unhappy about going anywhere near the thing, would not venture an opinion.

Kelling and Shaw came back then. They had rope and electric lanterns.

"You," Shaw told Dr Furrisky, "stay here." Furrisky's relief died when Shaw demanded her mobile phone. "There's no calling the police when we're down there. There's no landline in the house, so you give me your mobile."

Shaw had brought her automatic

submachine gun thing with her as well, and she got what she wanted. "Right," she said. "The four of us are heading down to see what this is about. Keep that bloody door open. If you think we can't push it open with a bunch of furniture against it you're wrong."

The thought had obviously not occurred to Dr Furrisky, who was looking less and less happy with the whole situation. Shaw shot her one more glare, and then handed me a lantern.

"Keep that lit, up over my shoulder," she told him. "Mr Psychic comes next, Kelling, rearguard."

The big man nodded. That he was rearguard against any pangs of civic duty Dr Furrisky might suffer was plain to all.

The doctor had sat down on the sofa now, looking utterly miserable, mixed up in something she plainly wanted nothing to do with.

"Let's go," Shaw said, and slipped down into the darkness.

I hurried after her, casting the lantern's light ahead down the steps, my eyes mostly on my own footing. The steps were not only steep and rounded, but shallow too: I slipped more than once. There was no railing, but the passage sides were close enough that I could drag myself straight on them. Shaw was more nimble, which was just as well as she had her gun in one hand and I didn't like to think of a stray shot bouncing about between the stone walls.

"Stop," Walther said, and we did, paused awkwardly on the steps. He had his own torch out, and was examining something on the walls. It was writing, scratched graffiti almost too faint to see, and not in English.

"Hell and all its devils await," Walther explained. "Latin, the church kind. We'll have to get Dr Furrisky to take a peek at it."

"Whatever." Shaw was not interested. When Walther spotted the next scrawling she barely stopped. There were several more, but Walther stopped reading them because they were no longer in Latin but in some scratchy, curly stuff that he could not decipher. Then we came to the door.

We had gone a long way down. I

reckoned we had been making our way now for about fifteen minutes, going carefully. Whatever we had expected, it was not this. The lantern made out two great stone slabs that blocked our way. They seemed to fit flush, and they had been carved all over, in squiggles and lines and knotwork all kind of joined together so that the entire face of them was a single big, random-looking design. Time and use had rubbed a lot away for all it had been cut deep into the stone.

I did not really look at the doors after that first time. I wonder now whether those marks were as random and abstract as I thought or whether, seen through different eyes, they might have made words, or even pictures. It is hard to know what to think, given what we saw later.

We did not even see them quite as doors, until Shaw pushed at one and it shifted. She jumped back hurriedly, but we had all seen a brief line of light when the door moved. They led outside.

"Must go all the way to the sea?" Shaw said uncertainly. "You got those tide tables?"

"We can't have come down far enough," Walther disagreed.

Shaw made a decision. "You two get behind Kelling and me," she said, and we made the adjustments with difficulty in the narrow stairwell. She and the big man exchanged some kind of unspoken signal, and then he put his shoulder to the doors, expecting resistance. They opened almost immediately, though, and he tumbled through. I heard weights slide in the walls beside me, a perfect counterbalance.

The light struck us, and so did the heat, a blast-furnace of it after the chill stone stairway. I covered my eyes, thinking of that Latin warning we had passed. Welcome to hell? It was a wet heat, too, and in a second my clothes were plastered to me, my body sweating itself into overdrive and the sweat having nowhere to go.

With the heat came the smell. I had a hint of it when Walther opened the secret door above, but it was here in spades. It was not a bad smell, just a strong and strange one. It smelt of the sea and fish, but with all sorts of other stuff mixed in.

For a moment I just swayed on my feet, one hand to the stone wall, trying to adjust. I opened my eyes.

It was the sea. The sun was very bright, far too bright, but it was the sea. In fact there was only the smallest strip of beach, barely two feet of stony shingle, before the water started. In the bright light the sea looked very blue, like an advert for a holiday resort in the Med or something. I could see fish in it, which was more than the sea normally showed you. There was a mist out on the sea still, despite the heat, or perhaps it was because of it. The air was very muggy, cloudy with condensation.

Walther had his hands to his ears, and I could see him swallowing repeatedly, leaning back against the passage wall.

"Just like being in a plane or something," he explained, looking annoyed, "like the pressure's suddenly dropped." He loosened the top two buttons of his shirt, which was unprecedented. Then he took off his jacket entirely.

Shaw and Kelling had ventured onto the narrow beach, both with guns in hand. I wondered if they had seen service in heat like this before. To me it was outlandish. It might have been July, but it was still Scotland.

"What the hell is going on?" I demanded.

Walther shook his head, without an answer for now. He was thinking, though, putting it together. I had faith in him.

I took a few steps along the beach in

the other direction. There were seabirds crying shrilly overhead on the cliffs. I peered up but the rock overhung us.

"Here!" I heard Shaw say, and made my uncertain way down the beach towards her. Walther was still in the doorway, staring out to sea. "Don't go far," he warned me.

Shaw had found a boat. It had been under a tarpaulin ten yards from the doors, where the beach was a little wider. I saw a rubber dinghy of faded yellow, complete with oars. It could have sat about four at a squeeze but one man could have rowed it, and I guessed that the one man was Dr Hendry.

There was a crate there too, and Shaw was busy levering off the top. Inside were batteries, dried food, some pills, matches, a miscellany of survival gear plus something peasant's-revolt-looking that turned out to be a boathook.

"Hendry's boat," Kelling said. "Accident?"

"The boat's still here," Shaw pointed out. "Unless he went swimming and got cramp it doesn't help us."

"Would you all come over here please?" Walther called. He sounded strained. I went straight off, and the other two sauntered after, looking suspicious.

Walther was pointing out to sea. "Do you see it?" he asked. His face was unreadable.

"Just mist," said Shaw.

"No, look," Walther insisted.

The mist was less than it had been. I looked, seeing only a big shark-looking fish in the near water, going about its business. Walther's arm was pointing further out, though, and I saw.

Shaw cursed at the same time, so I knew she'd seen it. There were shapes out there, now that the mist was fading.

"Michael, when you were looking this house up on the woo-wa, did you find anything on those?" Walther asked.

I hadn't. It was always the problem with the internet. It gave you exactly what you asked for, and would never mention, as a human would, "And did you hear about the ships?"

There were ships out there, in the

muggy mist. I counted at least four that I could see, great grey shadows in the gloom. They were not modern ships. I saw the masts, the tattered rigging. They were ghosts, it seemed, ancient and insubstantial. If we had seen skeletons about the ropes of them I wouldn't have been surprised.

"I make the big one a galleon, perhaps a Spaniard," Walther murmured. "And the long, low one could be a galley from a thousand years before. And maybe that one's a longship, a Viking raider. Good lord, we must get Dr. Furrisky down here to see them."

Shaw and Kelling were looking stubborn, and it was clear they had no idea what he was talking about.

"We should return to the house," Walther said. "We should look at what we've learned, make plans."

In the face of those spectral ships there was no argument.

"Ships?" Dr Furrisky said. "What, real ships?"

"Insofar as I could see," Walther confirmed.

"Hendry was building, what, fake ships?"

"I don't think so," Walther said.

"Only I found..." She grimaced. "I went over his study. I wanted proof of what he was doing. I found... more fakes."

"Fakes..." Walther let the word hang.

"Journals. There are three of them. One's English, circa seventeen hundred. Then there are some vellums of ecclesiastical Latin. The last I think is Dutch, but I don't read it so I can't be sure. But they're like everything else. They're all—"

"Too new," Walther finished. He had her sat down in the living room, the better to break the news. "Yes, well, we may have to revise our ideas of precisely what Mr Hendry was doing, Doctor."

Shaw and Kelling were back at their van, gathering more equipment. They were going to make a more determined expedition downstairs, I gathered.

The internet was being obliging. "I

have a newspaper report here from eighty-three. Some millionaire's yacht disappeared off the coast here. And they say that the place has been a real blackspot for shipping. Lots of disappearances. They call it a Scottish Bermuda Triangle."

"Being the press, of course they do. And I'm sure they say a lot about rocks and currents and winds. I'll bet they didn't find any wreckage, though."

I skipped from site to site. "There's quite a lot on it – Fortean Times gives it a mention. More Bermuda Triangle stuff. Goes way back. This one says there are folk tales about it."

"Find them for me," Walther said.

I tried for over an hour, while Walther

took Dr Furrisky down the stairs to the impossibly tropical beach and brought her back white-faced and shaking. As so often happens, I dug back to a point in time when nothing had been made electronic, and the sources I was referred to had never been uploaded.

"I don't understand," Furrisky was saying.

"This is no normal missing person matter, or even a criminal forging ring," Walther said. He was flicking through the papers we had found. "That is why we were all called in. Someone else knows that there's a singularity here." He didn't mean a black hole like the scientists or Star Trek would. In his trade it just means a happening, something odd.

"We're going down," Shaw announced, striding in. She and Kelling had packs on, and were armed to the teeth. Kelling even had two little pineapple-looking grenades on his belt.

"I wouldn't advise it," Walther said absently.

"So? We'll do a complete sweep of the beach, see if there's a trail up the cliffs. Then we'll go out to the ships."

Walther shrugged. "I'm sure I can't stop you," he said mildly, which meant to me that he was up to something. The two ex-soldiers clumped off down the stone stairs.

"I don't know what to think," Dr Furrisky got out.

"That's a good starting point," Walther

conceded. "We will need to examine those ships, sooner or later. Preferably later, by my reckoning."

"But—"

"Tell me about your journals, please."

Dr. Furrisky made a visible effort to calm herself. "Well… the English one is supposed to have been written by a Captain John Marlough of the Sarah May, which seems to have been trading in wool out of Boston. There's a lot of – well there's a lot of detail."

I didn't understand why she was looking so distressed until Walther said, "I think we can assume that the diary is genuine, Dr. Furrisky."

"But…"

"Despite its apparent condition. And so, mundane detail is just what one would expect. Please go on."

Dr. Furrisky had the journal with her, a little leather-bound thing close-written in cramped handwriting. I got a look at it and could recognise only a few words of the English. "Well there was a storm. This was the 16th of September 1693 by his reckoning. They were blown off course."

"Indeed," Walther said.

"Then they found... well they mention the heat, and they were becalmed. They talk about other ships. Rations running low. They say the other ships were abandoned. And they say..."

Walther leant forwards.

"Captain Marlough says there were

monsters in the sea, that his crew saw. Here: 'Garley says he saw a great monster of the sea while on watch at the third bell once more, like to a turtle and a whale.' The captain doesn't believe it but, two days later he sees one himself, in plain daylight, or he says he does."

Walther's eyes were very narrow. "Monsters," he said simply.

"And – there's not much more, you see. He just... it's two weeks after they were becalmed and he just says, 'This sea is inhabited by devils.' And that's all."

Walther nodded. "Michael, come downstairs with me briefly, will you?" He got up without warning and went into the cool passageway, and with a shrug at Dr Furrisky I followed.

We clattered down the stone steps, and I was surprised how long it was before we saw any light from below, and even longer before we felt any of the heat. Still, when we got out it was just as before, the hammer-blow of the sun, the misty sea with its great corpses of ships, and the narrow shingle of the beach. Shaw and Kelling were down a ways, and I saw they had the rubber dinghy by the water's edge.

"Excuse me, but I think you should come in now," Walther said politely.

"Is that right?" Shaw scowled at him.

"It really is," Walther confirmed. "Call it a hunch."

"Listen," she told him. "I know you. You're no psychic. I seen nothing to show you're any kind of psychic. All you've done is find a door, that anyone could have found. Now you can shut up and get your money when we go back, but as far as I care you're in no position to give orders."

"I'm just making a friendly suggestion," Walther said. "Perhaps you should come back into the house and we can go and look at the ships together a bit later."

"Your assistance ain't required," Kelling rumbled.

"Go back up," Shaw told us.

"Come with us," Walther said.

"Right." Abruptly she had a pistol in one hand. "Listen you. If I decide to lay you out right now, you think anyone'll even find the body?"

"No," said Walther sadly. "I'm fairly sure they won't."

"Then you just let us do our job," she said.

"Very well." We went back in without another word, climbing the steps all the way up to the house. Walther had an odd look on his face when we got to the top. Looking back on it, I cannot say how much of it he intended, or just what he had planned.

"What about the Latin?" he asked Dr Furrisky, as though they had never been interrupted.

"There's no name or year. I'd think from the usage it's a monk of some kind, and maybe around the thirteenth century. He mentions setting sail from the Humber, bound for a monastery he doesn't bother naming. Again there's a storm, and he says he sees the sky change colour. He… thinks it's the second coming, judgment day. So he thinks where the ship goes is… hell."

"Complete with devils."

"Yes," she said. "Devils that eat the crew, or take them into the water."

Walther stood up suddenly. I thought it was what the doctor had said, but he had a hand out as though listening. When he saw us looking blankly at him he frowned. "Did you hear that?"

We had heard nothing, and Walther nodded. "Michael, time to go downstairs again."

He lit one of the electric lanterns this time, and we trooped all the way down once more, and I was still wondering why it seemed further this time, when we reached the end. There was no light from below. There was no carven door. The passage ended in sheer stone.

In the back of Hendry's ledger, Walther explained, there were formulae. They were not Hendry's. They matched the handwriting of whoever had started the ledger in the nineteen-twenties. "I do not know what data informs the formulae," Walther explained. "It may be astrological, I cannot say without further study. They are used to calculate times and dates, however. They are singularly precise, and Doctor Hendry found them important enough to make these calculations over and over and over, hundreds of pages of them."

"But calculating what?" Doctor Furrisky demanded.

"When that door below us is open, and when it is not."

A silence fell on the sitting room. The secret door had been pushed to, out of some odd measure of respect.

"Let me explain my hypothesis, which we shall have the benefit of testing in precisely eight hours and thirty-one minutes," Walther explained. "The passageway there does not lead to the bottom of the cliff, or not in any conventional sense. It simply does not go down far enough. My sense for such things is very acute. The doorway at the end of the passage leads..."

"To the foot of the cliff," said Dr. Furrisky stubbornly.

"To the foot of a cliff," Walther corrected. "Where it is much hotter. Where conditions are very different."

"Where there are devils?" I asked. I was unsure whether I was doubting him or not.

"Anything is possible," he said. "I would also theorise that similar portals open sporadically at sea off these cliffs, large enough that the occasional luckless vessel is taken through, hence our ghost-ships."

"And Dr Hendry?" I said. "He missed his chance? Got stuck there?" With the monsters and devils, my mind added.

"I'm not sure," said Walther. "Because he seems to have been very careful about these calculations. That's the one piece that doesn't quite fit. However, I would suggest we all get a little sleep over the next few hours. When we go down again, we'll make a proper expedition of it."

"But what about the others?" Dr Furrisky asked him.

Walther and I exchanged glances.

"He tried to get them to come back,"

I said, thinking, But he never told them why.

In the morning we got ready as best we could. We bundled all the useful stuff we found around the house into rucksacks – food, lamps, tools – and, after a lot of thought, I took a pistol from Shaw's van. It had been a long time since I'd held one, and I didn't like it, but I liked what we might be going into even less.

The doors were there again when we got down. We did not get to see that moment of disconnection, when the bare stone wall became the elaborately carved portal. We pushed through, into the intolerable, sapping heat, looking for

Shaw and Kelling. I kept the gun handy and carefully did not think about whether it was Shaw and Kelling I had brought it for, if they decided they had been hard done by.

There was no immediate sign of them. For a moment we just stood by the door, trying to get used to the heat again. I shrugged the pack off, even the straps over my shoulders becoming unbearable insulation.

What we found was by Hendry's boat, where the beach was a little wider. That was where they had gone, in the end. The foot of the cliff still bore some red marks including a handprint. There were scraps of clothing. One remaining boot, Kelling's from the size, proved still to have a foot in it. That was enough for

Dr Furrisky, who threw up against the cliff-base.

Walther sighed, a man whose theory is proven right rather savagely. He had brought his umbrella, and now he poked about with it and I saw there were bones left too, but they were in pieces, cracked and fractured into shards. There were still some crabs and things crawling about, looking for the last few scraps.

"My God, what happened to them?" Dr Furrisky asked weakly. In truth we could not be sure that Shaw was not still alive. There was not enough left on the beach to make a single body, let alone two. I don't think any of us had doubts, though.

Walther poked his umbrella-tip through a lace and lifted the occupied boot up fastidiously. It had been chewed, and the teeth of the chewer had been large and sharp, piercing the leather in big triangular wedges.

Something shiny caught my eye. Shell casings. Once I had seen the first I kept seeing them. It looked as though they had put up a fight, for what it was worth.

"We have eleven hours and some minutes to make our investigation," Walther said. "Although looking at the sun suggests it will be dark by then anyway."

"And after that time...?" I asked.

"The door will be gone again."

"And the monsters will come out?"

Walther gave me an odd look, the sort given to a slow learner. "The monsters are already here, Michael. We just won't have anywhere to run to. Now, I suggest we get out to the ships while we can."

I saw something then, because I was trying not to look at what little was left of Shaw and Kelling. Down the beach, where it got rockier, something dark slid off into the sea. The movement was all I saw, and I told myself it was a seal, because what else could it have been? The memory of that motion stayed with me though. There had been something unpleasantly boneless about the way it had slumped into the water.

Nobody except Walther wanted to go out to the ships, but he convinced us.

He made it clear that there was no other way we were going to be able to complete our work here, and that was something both Dr Furrisky and I wanted to do as quickly as possible. We all three of us got into Hendry's dinghy, going knee-deep in the warm water to launch it. Yours truly got to row us out, of course, with Walther sitting at the front giving a constant stream of directions to my back.

He aimed us for the nearest ship, some kind of galleon. Looking over my shoulder I could see its curved wooden side rising like a wall. Above that the sails were holed and mouldering. I reckoned it had been there a while, and then I wondered how many more than we could see were already sunk on the bottom beneath us, their secrets gone forever.

"Not that one. Left, Michael, turn left," Walther said. Despite the ever-present mug of the mist he had spotted something colourful.

I did what he asked, straining away at the oars, my arms and back starting to burn with the work. I had to stop and drain one of our water bottles. I felt that I'd sweated out my entire bodyweight, and the air was so wet the sweat was just sitting there refusing to go anywhere. I don't think I've ever felt so tired.

"There!" Walther said triumphantly. We were grazing alongside one of the ships now, so that Dr Furrisky had to fend it off with the boathook. I was too tired to care where we were going then, so it was only when Walther told me to stop rowing that I saw what had caught his eye. It was a rope, perhaps the very climbing rope whose packaging we had found. It was slung all the way up over the rail, and there were knots in it to make it easy to climb.

"Do you think... Hendry's up there?" I asked, and Walther gave me a scathing look, until I remembered that if Hendry was on the ship, he had somehow managed to send his dinghy back to shore and get it to stow itself. This is why Walther does the investigating and I do the manual labour.

"Up," said Walther, but I had to rest first, drinking more water and letting my muscles ease. Eventually, whilst Walther fretted, I was ready to go, and I went first, with the gun shoved through my belt like an American detective. It was an easy climb, after all that. Hendry had known his stuff, with ropes and knots and the like. This ship was lower at the middle than the first one we had gone for, although it had whole great castle-looking things at each end. When I was on deck I looked about, but there was nobody, of course.

I helped the other two up. Dr Furrisky's face had gone very strange. I reckon that the ship was beyond her ability to claim as a fake. She hadn't really believed, until she set foot on it.

"It's a carrack," she said. I thought she said 'carrot' the first time, but Walther explained it was a kind of ship.

She was looking up at the sails, which were mostly whole, trying to see what the little flag was at the top. There was no wind, though, and everything was hanging slack.

"It must be new here," Walther said. "I'm guessing the heat and humidity speeds up the rate of decay. The sails on all the others are just shreds, and I wouldn't want to trust the wood, for that matter." He stamped, hollow on the deck. "I imagine Hendry gets aboard as quickly as possible to collect his souvenirs."

"But what about all the sailors?" I asked. I could see Furrisky hadn't thought about it – she was used to historical artefacts coming uninhabited. Walther was nodding, though.

"No sign of anyone. Marie Celeste, you might say." There was a square hatch to belowdecks, but it was open and Walther shone his torch down it. "Sacks of something," he reported. "Whatever they were carrying."

Dr Furrisky had found a proper door, though it was so low even Walther had to stoop under it. It led to whatever part of below the people had lived in. Everything was very cramped, and the air was baking and stale. There was a big room that I guessed the crew had lived in, and there were still bags and things roped to the sides. There were a couple of smaller rooms too, with open doors. A lot of junk was still scattered about. There was no sign of anyone.

"Here," Walther said. Everything was torch work, of course. Save for the little light from the open door it was pitch down there. Walther had illuminated some stains about one of the smaller rooms. They looked like they were blood, dried on. They were all over a little bunk there, on the woollen sheets, straw mattress and over the walls too. I began to feel trapped, all sort of closed-in by the walls and ceiling.

Walther was shining his torch at the open door now, and I saw that it had been bolted on the inside, at one time. The bolt was iron, and it was bent into a curve, as though something had put a great deal of slow and patient pressure on it.

We got back up top quickly enough. We were all a bit shaky, I think. Nobody wanted to talk about it right then, and because of what happened next we never really did. I've thought about it, though. In fact, it keeps coming back to me.

Walther checked his watch and declared we should head back, so we scrambled down into the little boat again and I began to row for shore. We were about halfway back when it happened.

I should say it was getting darker by then. The sun was over the cliffs. It wasn't night or anything, but we didn't see it as clearly as we might.

It came to investigate the boat. Dr Furrisky saw it first and called out, pointing. I saw a shadow pass under us, big and dark. I thought it was a dolphin or something, but it was bigger than that. Of course I was rowing, so there wasn't much I could do about it, but I saw it pass behind the boat and then curve round for us again, slowing. It was longer than our dinghy, but it nudged us delicately, carefully, obviously not really sure what we were or whether to eat us.

It was long in the water, and it had a head with jaws like a crocodile, but it had flippers, too. I could see them clearly as it held its place in the water, bumping forward into us. I just kept rowing.

It came alongside us, and the head lifted from the water a little. It had a very small eye on the side of its head, and lots and lots of teeth that seemed to stick out any old how.

"Well," said Walther softly. I could see he was not scared, just very impressed.

I just kept rowing, doing my best not to prod the thing with an oar. A moment later it went under, and I thought it might come up beneath us and turn us over, but it was gone.

We got back to shore and hurried up the stairs. Nobody wanted to be trapped like Shaw and Kelling.

"I think we can make our report now," Walther said. We just stared at him. He closed the door to the passageway and then, with some effort, shoved the sofa back against it.

"This is not my area of expertise," he said flatly. "There are no ghosts here, no spirits. In fact the lack of ghosts is what has been bothering me. I had not realised how used I was to the constant pressure of them, everywhere, layer on layer, until I found somewhere they were not."

"But the ships—" I said.

"As real a you or I, as is the place. Just not our place, Michael, and a foolish place for Mr Hendry to play with, a dangerous hobby."

Dr Furrisky went to sit on the sofa, but didn't. In fact we were all giving it a wide berth just through association. "Where were we down there?" she demanded. "We all know that if we found our way down the cliffs outside we'd not find that heat. We'd not see those ships."

Walther nodded. "Holes in space," he said. "There is evidence. There are other accounts. Holes in space and time. The door below, that is a predictable one. Whether the holes out at sea that have snared so many ships are, who can say? But yes, it all leads elsewhere." He shook his head, wonderingly. "I think our inquisitive friend at sea was a pliosaur, at best guess, which would mean that our passage under the stairs goes back about... a hundred million years."

"But the ships..." Dr Furrisky said.

"The ships, the luckless ships, dragged into the baking heat of an age when their most distant ancestors were little marsupial mice. What can they have thought, in the brief time they had? They thought it was hell, and who can blame them?"

"But what happened to them?" she asked.

"It would be nice to think that if we had reached the top of those cliffs we might have found some little stockaded village of Vikings and Romans and Dutch merchants, using spears and muskets to ward off the brachiosaurs," Walther said, and it was clear he didn't believe it. "However I think they met the same fate as our erstwhile comrades. The Jurassic is a dangerous place to be out in." He met my gaze then, and so I did not say what I was going to say, about just how likely I thought it that dinosaurs would get on the ships and force open cabin doors.

We made our report. No comment

was raised about the loss of Shaw and Kelling, and we got our money, prompt and in cash. Officially it was the last we knew of it, but Walther has sources, and he told me later that a report was doing the rounds, of some of the things found in Hendry's house. The shells and the fish skeletons were all new species, unknown to science. They never knew, I'd guess, that Walther and I had walked off with the tub of silver coins. I reckon Dr Furrisky took a few souvenirs as well.

Walther and I didn't talk much about what happened, or what might have happened, either on the ships or to Mr Hendry. There was this unspoken idea that it was just the dinosaurs, or whatever, that did for everyone. That's what we put in our report.

I can't stop thinking about those doors, though: the big stone doors at the end of the passage, that were carved in all those squiggles and lines. Mostly, I think about the fact that they were on the other side of the doorway, that when the time-door or whatever was closed, those doors were still in the Jurassic. I think about that, and the way that the ships had been cleared of crew so completely, and then I think about the thing I saw sliding off the rocks into the sea, when we found what was left of Shaw and Kelling. It comes back to me in my nightmares, that: the boneless slump of it into the water. I think about what Mr Hendry might have taken from the sea, for his fish tank, and whether, to reclaim it, something might have come up from that doorway, something that took Mr Hendry, too, because I am more and more sure that he did not just miss the doorway and die on the beach. I wonder, then, whether there wasn't more about the Jurassic that we know. I've read about fossils, and how little we really know, especially about squid-like things that have no bones and leave few traces.

And when I get as far as that I just hope, really hope, that the Hendry house falls into the sea sooner rather than later, because some things should stay extinct.

About the Author

Adrian Tchaikovsky is an award-winning British fantasy and science fiction author. He is a keen live role-player, occasional amateur actor, and has trained in stage-fighting.

He has written over 20 novels and won the 2016 Arthur C. Clarke Award for *Children of Time* and the 2017 British Fantasy Award — Best Fantasy Novel for *The Tiger and the Wolf*.

We would like to thank everyone who made this project possible,
via the Kickstarter and outside of it.

Specific thanks goes to:

Aaron Armitage

David Parker

Ross Warren

More dyslexic friendly

titles coming soon...